MW00914227

KARAOKE
Sing Along Guide To Fun & Confidence

KARAOKE

Sing Along Guide To Fun & Confidence

Scott Shirai

Visual Perspectives
P.O. Box 459
Honolulu, Hawaii 96809-0459
(808) 566-0084

For information, contact:
Visual Perspectives
P.O. Box 459
Honolulu, Hawaii 96809-0459
e-mail: karaokeu@hits.com

Cover Design: DeWayne Sluss
Graphics: Deron Furukawa, Kevin Doyle
Editor: Michelle M. Jerin

ISBN 0-9654864-0-0

To my dad, George Y. Matsuoka,
who instilled the love of music within me.

Contents

Acknowledgments

With special thanks to my hundreds of students, and heart-felt appreciation to Michelle M. Jerin for her inspiration and enduring friendship through countless hours of editing and design.

To Sharon Narimatsu for launching my career teaching karaoke at the college level, Kisaburo "Kay" Takagi for his unwavering support and input, Dr. Ray Oshiro, program specialist at the University of Hawaii, for having faith in my classes, Ben Fong-Torres, Paulette Feeney, Carole Kai and Dennis Enomoto of Hawaii Stars Studios for their ongoing support, Don and Bob Iinuma of Hawaii Multimedia Center for their steadfast encouragement and help, and to Ed Sanders for teaching me lyric analysis.

To Suzanne Lanouye, Mona Wood, Sandra Au Fong, Audrey Enseki Tom, Emiko Takada, Ron Arnone, John Lawrence, Katherine Williams, M.D., Michele Arakaki, Vincenzo Palleschi, Raphael Pungin, Nancy Hansen, Ron Nishiki, Rogene Talento, Gerald Tossey, Walter Omori, Al Waterson, Nancy Bernal, Audy Kimura, Michael W. Perry, Larry Price, Kimo Kahoano, David "Kawika" Talisman, Doc Laing, and Phil Mow for their help on this project and invaluable contributions to this book.

Foreword

I first became acquainted with karaoke around 1980 while living at the time in Honolulu. This was after I had wrapped up the *Happy Days* television series and before I got involved with the *Karate Kid* movies. I had been playing softball in a *makule* (Hawaiian for old-timer) league and, after a game, some of my friends took me to a neighborhood bar that featured a great sounding karaoke system and free, delicious ethnic *pupus* - Hawaiian for hors d'oeuvres. I've been fascinated with karaoke ever since and now even have my own home karaoke system, given to me as a wedding present by a good friend, Mr. Mark Makabe, of Pioneer Electronics.

When I was first introduced to karaoke, most of the songs were Japanese. One of my favorites and a number in which I later appeared on a karaoke laser disc, is *Kokoni Sachi Ari* (Here is Happiness). Since then, there's been an explosion of recordings and there are now thousands of songs available in a variety of languages. In my travels, I've discovered that karaoke is not only becoming internationally accepted, but that it's here to stay, especially in the Western world.

Until *The Karate Kid*, people knew me mostly as a comedian, but starring in that movie and being nominated for an Oscar changed the perception of a lot of people. One of that movie's most powerful and touching scenes was one in which I was drunk in my bedroom and sang an old Japanese drinking song, *Urumachi Jinsei*, a tale about an alley orphan, to a photo of my deceased wife.

I had never considered myself a singer. I mean, I always liked music and love to sing with friends. But standing in front of a group of strangers, let alone in a movie before a worldwide audience, and singing a song can be a most nerve wracking experience, ranking even higher in stress than public speaking, if one allows that sort of thing to get to one.

And you know, as a kid in school, I still recall how nervous I would get whenever I had to stand in front of the class and recite the pledge of allegiance or the preamble to our constitution. It was as if I was standing there *hadaka* - Japanese for naked.

Of the American karaoke numbers, high on my list of favorites are songs by the legendary Nat King Cole. I've also been learning a few Hawaiian tunes on my visits to Hawaii.

Music has always been important to me. As a kid whose family was sent off to an internment camp with thousands of others after the Japanese bombed Pearl Harbor, songs were the glue that helped hold us together. Music is indeed a universal language that transcends all borders, countries, tongues and times.

My friend, Scott Shirai's book, *Karaoke: Sing Along Guide To Fun & Confidence*, says it all. Not only does it describe the hardship of standing before others, but it also contains easy tips and exercises for singing better, and the book will help bolster your confidence. And let me tell you, if you can sing in front of people, you'll have no problem whatsoever whenever you have to speak or make a presentation before others.

And through karaoke, music can be a valuable tool that enables people to stand confidently, to rise above that moment of terror, and to find their own interpretive selves.

Karaoke helps create an atmosphere of fun and can also be an enormous social asset. Some people laugh and think I'm kidding when I say that there ought to be karaoke systems on every school campus and in every retirement center. That's true and that's no joke!

Let's all enjoy and say, "OKAY TO KARA-O-KAY."

Pat Morita

Author's Note

Have you ever discovered that doing a favor can sometimes lead to a most rewarding, if not, unusual and unexpected experience? That happened to me several years ago. A friend of mine who was in charge of non-credit courses at a local community college called me and asked for a favor. Without hesitation, I said, "Sure."

It turned out that the college had scheduled a karaoke course but the instructor quit before classes even started. My friend thought of me because she remembered that I had majored in voice in college, and probably because she also knew I would agree to help her before asking what the favor was. She was right on both counts.

That was in 1989 and since then, I've taught hundreds of people to have fun and feel more confident through karaoke. Oahu's evening newspaper, the *Honolulu Star-Bulletin*, even labeled my courses *KARAOKE U.*

I have witnessed people transform from timid wallflowers to bold, self-assured singers. Who could have guessed that the confidence from singing would also be transferred to their everyday lives and work? One student told me how this newly-found confidence has helped him close more real estate sales. Another discovered that she was no longer afraid to deliver speeches before strangers. These are just a few of countless success stories.

Up until about 1993, if you had asked me what kind of people signed up for my classes, I would have replied instantly that they were all over 60 years old and of Japanese descent. Since then, I've observed scores of people from 8 to

80 years old and from every ethnic group enroll in my classes. The classes are so popular that there are often waiting lists. People attend my classes for a variety of reasons. Some want to be successful in contests and performing on stage while others simply want to learn more about this fast-growing hobby. Many just want to sound better, feel more confident, and make new friends.

The karaoke explosion continues to rumble across the country. My talks with representatives of leading karaoke publications and song distributors confirm that karaoke is here to stay.

Through my classes, I've seen and have been moved by the positive changes that karaoke brought to hundreds of my students. I'd like to share that same knowledge and excitement with you.

KEY POINT: You may want to read this book cover to cover or go directly to those chapters which you think will help you the most. Look for those places I've labeled *KEY POINTS:* they're tips worth remembering or trying. But above all, I hope you'll have fun and feel more confident singing karaoke after you've read my book.

Chapter 1
Can I Sing Or Am I Really Tone Deaf?

"I don't know anything about music.
In my line, you don't have to."
- Elvis Presley -

Since I started teaching karaoke in 1989, I've been asked repeatedly, "Can you teach me to sing or am I tone deaf?" My answer is and has always been, "Yes, I can. If there is nothing wrong with your hearing, you can learn how to sing."

Okay, so you're probably saying, "Sure, I can hear, but I still can't sing and I certainly don't sound anything like Elton John, Mariah Carey or Frank Sinatra." The answer is simple. In order to sing properly, you must first be able to hear. Second, you need to understand what you're hearing, and finally, you must learn the secrets to unlock your voice.

Don't worry if this sounds a bit confusing. The examples in this book will help you understand what you're hearing and the exercises will arm you with skills to sing better. The power to sing well lies within you and I'd like to help you unleash that hidden potential.

Nearly all of my students show marked improvement after only two or three classes when they conscientiously apply my tips and advice. Many sign up for more classes to maintain their level of singing or to continue improving their techniques.

If you want to sound better, it will take teamwork. I'll share with you all the time-tested skills and tips I've taught hundreds of students. We'll learn the basics of singing - breathing, support and a free tone. And we'll explore other extras like vibrato and volume control. You'll need to make the commitment to try. The result: You will sing better and feel more confident doing it. Deal?

Teaching someone to sing can sometimes be frustrating. It is one of life's biggest challenges because an instructor has to successfully communicate numerous abstract concepts to a student. So stay with me when I ask you to try certain things like blowing up a balloon or singing to a candle. I promise you won't regret it.

You may be able to teach someone to sew or bowl through demonstration, but singing requires that each individual feel sensations and hear tones on his or her own. That's also why hearing - *critical hearing* - is essential.

Let me share with you one example. Once, while in Hilo, Hawaii to conduct a series of karaoke classes at Hawaii Stars Studios, I met and trained a shy 8-year-old who had never taken formal voice lessons. She was amazing! She belted out Whitney Houston and Mariah Carey songs with ease. And, guess what? She learned to sing those songs so well just by listening and mimicking the tones and styles she heard on the CDs.

You can learn the same skills. Listening not only applies to being able to sing well, but it is essential for impressionists. For example, internationally known impressionist Rich Little is so successful because he has the great ability to hear well and adapt his voice to the person he's mimicking.

KEY POINT: Watch as many singers as you can. Listen critically and become more aware of what you're hearing.

Hawaii has a half-hour karaoke show, *Hawaii Stars*, televised every Sunday evening. I have my karaoke students watch the show so we can discuss what they've heard and seen in the next class. If there's no locally televised karaoke show in your city, tune in to MTV or VH1 or any of the music video channels on your cable television.

You probably bought this book to improve your singing and to feel more confident in front of others. Well, the best way to get on the road to achieving both goals is to get out there and sing. Sing whenever and wherever you can. And when you're not out singing with others, practice. Practice a lot!

As an avid tennis player, I understand the importance of practice. And for me, I'd rather be on the court slamming a ball toward an opponent, than practicing solo against a backboard. Voice training is no different. A lot of students would rather come to class to work out vocally than practice on their own. One of my students holds the record of enrolling in five courses.

KEY POINT SUMMARY

Before moving ahead, try this: Tape yourself singing a song. Mark the tape with the date and put it away. Then, after reading my book and implementing the suggestions, tape yourself singing that same song again. Listen closely to both recordings. I believe you'll hear a difference that will please you.

Chapter 2
Who Lit The Fuse To The Karaoke Explosion?

"You can do anything you want to do
if you know what to do."
- Betty Carter -

I love to travel and whenever I'm on the road, I notice more and more karaoke bars and "boxes;" privately-equipped karaoke rooms for rent. From business men and women, to teens and seniors, the karaoke explosion continues to reverberate across the globe. But who lit the fuse?

Just ask someone where the concept of karaoke started. They will be quick to tell you, "Japan," when in fact the answer might be Boston, Massachusetts. Yes, Boston, home of the infamous tea party and Paul Revere's midnight ride

However, everyone agrees that the word karaoke is Japanese in origin. It's actually the abbreviated combination of two words, "karappo" meaning empty and "okesutura" or orchestra; hence karaoke = empty orchestra.

ONE IF BY BAND, TWO IF IT'S A HIGH C
Some Westerners suggest that karaoke may have begun

around the turn of the 20th century in America with a technique called lantern slide images or stereopticon. It was developed in 1850 and, as the name indicates, light for the glass slide images is produced by lanterns and projected on a screen. In the fall of 1895, vaudeville entertainers Howard and Emerson used this new invention and sang songs illustrated with dissolving views, at Benjamin F. Keith's theatre in Boston.

The invention of silent movies appears to have caused the first evolution in karaoke. In 1903, song films became popular as moviegoers sang songs to the accompaniment of a giant Wurlitzer organ that could imitate several different instruments. A ball that bounced over the lyrics helped the audience keep their places in the songs. At the time, theatre owners thought that offering song films would help attract crowds and add the dimension of sound that was then missing from the silver screen.

A few years later, nickelodeons, the predecessor to karaoke boxes, began opening up around the U.S. For a nickel, people could enter small amusement halls to view silent movies and also participate in sing alongs. American karaoke continued to evolve as theatre owners built lavish movie palaces to attract patrons. An integral part of these palaces was the Wurlitzer organ and song films with the bouncing ball.

Song films also reflected the patriotic mood of America and the times. From the Spanish American War to the 1930s, song films inspired Americans with messages of hope and bravery.

The popularity of song films slowly faded away after the invention and acceptance of movies with sound. However, Americans' love of music and sing along continued to flourish. In the 1940s, record companies produced sing along records and sold them along with copies of the songs' lyrics. For the first time, people could fire up their record players or victrolas and sing along with prerecorded songs in the privacy of their homes.

Two decades later, recognizing the future and increasing popularity of a new invention called television, band leader Mitch Miller telecast yet another version of American karaoke on his show, *Sing Along With Mitch*. This 1960s show was simply a television adaptation of earlier song films. Viewers could tune in weekly to Mitch, gather in the living room around the television set, and sing along to a bouncing ball.

THE SUN ALSO RISES

Easterners, on the other hand, suggest that karaoke may have started at a snack bar in Kobe, Japan when the establishment's strolling guitarist failed to show up for work. Stranded without entertainment, the bar owner went home and taped musical accompaniment for patrons to sing along with.

Some Easterners may also argue that karaoke boxes first appeared in 1984 in a rice field in the countryside of Okayama Prefecture, just west of Japan's Kansai area. As the story goes, the first box was actually a converted railway freight car located in a rice field so that neighbors would not complain about the noise.

THE EVOLUTION

While there may be differing claims about karaoke's roots, it is universally acknowledged that the Japanese developed and sophisticated the technology that is enjoyed today by millions around the world. And the person credited as lighting the fuse to the modern karaoke explosion is Nikkodo's founder, Mr. Kisaburo "Kay" Takagi.

Takagi got the idea to invent a modern karaoke machine after observing that bar workers would tip street musicians 500 yen to sing along with them whenever business was slow. He concluded that if there was such a great interest in singing, clubs could generate even more business if a machine with recorded orchestra music existed. He also believed that he could invent such a machine that would charge only 100 yen a song and still be profitable.

Takagi, left, with Shirai

Takagi, founder of Nikkodo Co., Ltd., personally assembled about a dozen 8-track tape players with amplifiers and microphones. He then hired musicians from a nearby cabaret to play the accompaniments. Takagi found that by placing metal tape at the end of each song he could program the tapes to stop after each number. His machines sold out immediately! This was in 1978 and marked the beginning of modern day karaoke and the start of Nikkodo Co., Ltd.

Technology progressed but not without some problems. The '70s also brought cassette players equipped with variable speed controls and a microphone. By speeding up or slowing down the cassette, a vocalist could raise or lower the key of a song while singing along to printed lyrics.

But speeding up a tape usually resulted in musical accompaniment that resembled the background for Alvin and the Chipmunks, while slowing it down sounded more like a dirge or the symptoms of a portable cassette player with dying batteries.

Improvements in Japanese technology resulted in laser disc players and amplifiers that could digitally change the keys of songs. On some machines, you can change the key of the song by pressing the appropriate buttons on the microphone.

With the laser discs, words are superimposed on a television screen over a usually picturesque and moving background to music recorded in stereo. The words to the song are shaded in tempo with the music so that even the beginning singer knows when to sing each word. And if the song is in the wrong key, a simple touch of a button raises or lowers the key without affecting the original speed of the recording.

As karaoke grew in popularity, more manufacturers jumped aboard the proverbial bandwagon. The result was the refinement of the already popular compact disc or CD to a medium called CD plus graphics or CD+Gs. Like the laser disc, words are shown on a television screen and the quality of the sound is outstanding. Changing keys is also simple.

For the consumer, CD+Gs offer a less expensive option to the laser discs. The trade-off is that CDs have less storage capacity than the larger laser discs and lyrics are usually displayed over a stationary background.

An even later development is MIDI karaoke or karaoke on a personal computer. There are numerous sites on the Internet filled with familiar songs and not so familiar ones, mainly originals by aspiring composers that you can download. Whatever the form, karaoke is here to stay.

Now let's move on and start singing!

Chapter 3
A Solid Foundation

*"Great music is that which penetrates the ear with facility
and leaves the memory with difficulty.
Magical music never leaves the memory."*
- Sir Thomas Beecham -

The three keys to great singing are support, proper breathing, and an open throat. What is support? Famous opera star and one of the world's greatest tenors, Luciano Pavarotti, was once asked to describe proper support and replied that it was like a woman bearing down in labor. Except for women who've given birth, such a concept is usually difficult to understand.

KEY POINT: One way to achieve the sensation Pavarotti described is to blow up an ordinary party balloon while paying close attention to what's happening with your abdominal muscles. Feel the downward pressure? All my students try this exercise in their first class.

To achieve proper support while singing, you need to maintain steady pressure through the entire phrase while you're singing. You may release that support for a brief moment at the end of the phrase while you take a breath, and then grab

Blowing up a balloon demonstrates proper support.

hat support again before going on to sing the next phrase. f you're singing a fast song, you may not have time to re- ease your support; hold it and just take a breath between ɔhrases.

When students ask, "Where are the muscles that provide he support?" I share the following simple exercise: With ʏour palm facing up, place your index finger and middle inger under your last rib and cough. You should feel some ɔutward pressure against your fingertips. These are the nuscles you use for support.

A student demonstrates a simple exercise to find the muscles that provide support. With your palm facing up, place your index finger and middle finger under your last rib and cough. You should feel some outward pressure against your fingertips.

AIR!

Breathing, the second key to great singing, goes hand-in-hand with support. But proper breathing may actually be more difficult to understand at first than support.

I know you're wondering, "but don't we breathe automatically?" Yes, but not necessarily the proper way for singing. Remember your last visit to the doctor. You were asked to take a deep breath and responded by raising your shoulders and inhaling deeply. That is exactly how you *shouldn't* breathe for singing. By lifting your shoulders, your stomach rises into your chest area, tightening it up and constricting your throat.

KEY POINT: The proper way to breathe is quite different. What you want to do is to open up your chest cavity so that it can accept as much air as possible and allow the sound to resonate. That means pushing out and down on your stomach as you inhale. Doing so leaves more room for your lungs to expand.

Try that when you sing. In the beginning, it'll look and feel unusual and you'll have to consciously remind yourself to do it. But after awhile, it will become automatic.

If you ever learned to drive a stick-shift vehicle, it may have seemed impossible at first to remember all the things you had to do. But, after practice, patience and time, the mechanics of synchronizing the shifting became second nature. The same will happen to your breathing and support if you stick to it and practice.

KEY POINT: If you're still having difficulty envisioning what it's like to breathe properly, lie on the floor and take deep breaths while paying attention to what's happening with your abdomen. You should continue bearing down and when you take a breath, use both your mouth and nose. After all, you need as much air as possible.

Breathing is a lot like swimming. The more air you use, the bigger the breath you must take. Exercising proper breath control while singing a phrase is the key which I discuss in greater detail in Chapter 5.

In class, I remind my students that singing and sports are very similar. Like a good tennis serve, a good pitch, or strong breaststroke, a consistently good vocal tone is achieved by imitating previous good tones.

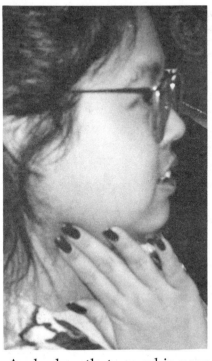

How is your sound produced? It's similar to playing a woodwind instrument in which air is blown over a reed causing it to vibrate. Here's another example. Remember blowing across the edge of a piece of paper as a kid to make a sound? A similar thing happens when you sing.

Now, take your index and middle finger, press it along the side of your throat and say, zzzzzz. The vibration you feel is that of air flowing over your vocal chords. This is what produces your sound. And when that sound is properly supported and on pitch, you usually have a pleasant tone.

SAY AH!

Ever wonder how babies and children can cry day and night and not lose their voices, while adults lose theirs after only a few minutes of cheering at a ball game? The kids are crying and screaming with open throats and supporting the wailing sounds with their abdominal muscles, while the cheering adults are forcing sounds from their throats.

An open throat is the third key component to successful singing after proper breathing and support. It is attained when the tip of your tongue is resting behind your front teeth and your jaw is dropped down and relaxed.

If you remember nothing else from my book but this, sing with an open throat. The consequences of not doing so are too painful. I had several people come to me for lessons after having operations to remove nodules in their throats. Those nodules were the result of improper singing

KEY POINT: If you sing with proper abdominal support and keep your jaw down and relaxed, you're not likely to have such problems. In fact, it's not uncommon at first to feel like you're exaggerating whenever you open your mouth and drop your jaw.

This is also what's referred to as a "free" tone. It's not easy at first, but like so many things in life, if you keep doing this for any length of time, it becomes second nature and you won't have to even think about it.

CRUNCH TIME

KEY POINT: Remember, singing and athletics are very similar. If you're serious about singing, get in shape. Visit your local gym or health club. Jog or enjoy other aerobic activities to build up your endurance and lung capacity. Do crunches and leg lifts to strengthen your abdominal muscles.

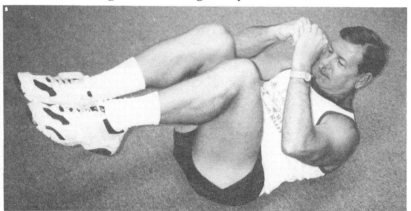

Not only will aerobics improve your singing, it's good for you. Before you embark on your Rocky-like quest, be sure to consult your doctor.

So with the proper support, good breath control and an open throat, you're all set to sing. But, don't quit your day job just yet to go on tour. These are just the foundations of good singing. There's still a lot more to learn.

Someone once approached famed Russian pianist Vladimir Horowitz and told him he would give anything to play like the maestro. Horowitz replied, "Yes, but would you be willing to practice eight hours a day?"

Practice really does make perfect if you want to excel in your singing.

KEY POINT SUMMARY

· Breathe using proper abdominal support.
· Bear down as you sing.
· Relax and drop your jaw for a "free" tone.
· Exercise.

Chapter 4
Hone, Hone On The Range

"Do or do not. There is no try."
- Yoda, The Empire Strikes Back -

In my mid 20s, I was a part of a group that sang musical jingles, the kind you hear on the radio and in television commercials. Singing jingles requires a good vocal range since the music is written by others and you have no control over the ranges or keys of the songs.

One day, unexpectedly, one of our female singers quit. We searched for a replacement for several weeks with no success until we heard of a 16-year-old student who was singing on weekends at local military clubs with two other teenagers.

After setting up a meeting and assuring her mother that I had no ulterior motives, I picked her up and drove to the home of our keyboard player where we put her through a variety of vocal exercises and songs. What a discovery, I initially thought, in hearing this rich, beautiful voice. To our dismay, however, this young woman had a limited vocal range. We reluctantly told this young girl with the velvety voice that she couldn't join our group and wished her well.

I had forgotten about her and the audition until several years later while sipping a hot cup of coffee and reading the newspaper. I came across a magnificent review of *Jesus Christ Superstar* and a new female discovery, Yvonne Elliman. Can you imagine my surprise? This was the girl we had turned away just a few years earlier! What's the point? The point is that recognizing your strengths and weaknesses and then choosing songs that fit you the best can make you sound better right away.

One of the keys to sounding good at karaoke requires people to understand their own voices and range, their strengths and weaknesses. Unless you've studied and practiced for years, it's unlikely that you have a range of 3 or 4 octaves, that is, singing from *do* up to *do*.

Be patient. If you're not a runner, you wouldn't attempt a marathon next week or next month without training and working up to it months prior, would you? People who train in martial arts do a lot of stretching exercises so that they can be flexible and capable of throwing high kicks. It takes years of stretching to achieve tournament flexibility. Training your voice and extending your range are no different.

INSTANT SUCCESS

In general, most people who start off singing karaoke choose familiar songs, ones that remind them of a special place or moment, or because they like the vocalist who recorded the song. That's good and understandable. But be careful. If you're singing or about to sing karaoke, many of the songs you select may be in keys that do not fit in your range.

Since I began teaching karaoke in 1989, I've logged the number of times I've had to change keys for students. I discovered that I change keys about 70 percent of the time.

In some cases, I change the key to put the song in a more comfortable range for the singer. They may be hitting the notes but not as solidly, so the sound isn't as good as it could be. Simply changing the key makes a noticeable difference. But in most instances, I change keys because the songs are in keys that are either too low or too high for the students. As in life and in sports, each of us has different capabilities. The trick is knowing what they are.

KEY POINT: The quickest improvement nearly every karaoke singer can make is to put songs in the key most perfect for them. If you have a limited range of say, one octave, then you should choose and sing songs that have a limited range.

Al, one of my former students, was referred to me because he was uncomfortable singing and lacked confidence. He was even more insecure because he was interested in expanding his business to Japan where it is typical to do business after hours at a box or karaoke bar. "I hardly ever sang as a kid. I thought I was tone deaf because I couldn't reach the same notes as the other kids," Al said.

But after listening to him sing a couple of songs and determining his range, I quickly discovered that Al was not tone deaf at all. In fact, he had a beautiful, rich baritone voice that was a fourth (four white piano keys) lower than most males.

It's no wonder that when he previously tried to sing with others, he would get discouraged because the songs were out of his range and not in his key. Now, Al changes the keys of nearly every song he sings, sounds great, and has even landed a Japanese client. He understands he's not tone deaf and has gained the confidence of a seasoned performer after only two months of private instruction and lots of practice.

How do you determine your range? Quite simple. Find a piano and sing the scale (*do, re, mi, fa,* etc.) starting at C. If the note is too low, just keep playing and start singing when it becomes comfortable for you.

Look at the picture below to see what note you start singing from and to. Sing each note as you play each white key while ascending the scale until you reach the next C, then keep going up until you can continue no more. If you started singing at the first C and were able to reach the next 2 C's, that means you have a 2-octave range.

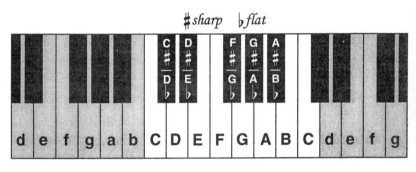

Similarly, if you began singing at C and were able to sing past the next C up to F, you have a range of about an octave and a half.

If you don't have access to a piano, you can get a fair idea of your range by singing songs with different ranges. *The Rose*, for example, suits someone with a limited range. *My Way* demands a greater range and *Music of the Night* an even wider one.

Armed with the knowledge of how wide or narrow your range is, look for songs that have a similar range - small, moderate, or wide. If in doubt, start with a small range and graduate to songs with wider and wider ranges as you feel more comfortable.

CHEST BECAUSE

By now, if you've been practicing the vocal exercises I suggested, you've probably noticed that the quality of your tones changes as you go up the scale. This is a natural effect. You were probably using chest tones while singing the lower notes and head tones for the higher ones.

Chest tones are distinguishable because of their fullness and richness; they take advantage of the resonance of our larger chest cavities. We use chest tones for lower notes.

Visualize for a moment that you are riding a runaway horse. You pull on the reins and yell *whoa* trying to get him to stop. From where did the sound emanate? Your chest, right?

Or, imagine you are a block away from your car when you notice someone about to vandalize it. You yell *hey* loudly. Where did that sound come from? Probably your chest. You wouldn't be very intimidating if you sounded like a boy soprano, would you?

IT'S GONE TO YOUR HEAD

Head tones, as the words imply, are produced primarily in the head. More specifically the mouth, sinus cavities, nose, and a little in the throat. Head tones are distinguished by a brighter sound. Imitate the hooting sound of an owl. That's a head tone.

Now, switch from saying *whoa* to hooting like an owl. Hear and feel the difference? From now on, whenever you listen to the radio or watch a singer on television, try to figure out if you're hearing a head or chest tone.

THE TRANSITION GAME

One of the areas in which many singers can improve is in the transition from a chest tone to a head tone or vice versa. Everyone makes the transition at a different place on the scale. That's normal. The trick is first finding out where that occurs and then making that transition smoothly.

Why is this important and why should you care? This smooth transition is important because most songs don't have large leaps - a big jump from one note to another. One exception is the beginning of *Over the Rainbow* with a one-octave leap while singing the first word of the song, "*Somewhere.......*"

Most songs are written with a leap of one or two or three steps between notes. So when a listener hears a great chest tone on one note and a great head tone on another, it can be subtly disconcerting because of the difference in tones. Smoothing out the transition makes you sound better.

If you're like me, you probably don't remember studying estuaries in school. But I wish I had. I've since found that estuaries - those inlets of water containing a mixture of salt and fresh water - are a lot like vocal transitions. A blend of both chest and head tones is important for that short, but important, transitional phase. And every singer's voice goes through such a transition.

Successful athletes make a similar change. In basketball, it's the transition game. In golf, the approach and, in tennis, coming to the net. Shifting from one phase to another requires a smooth change-over, whether in singing or in sports. That's what makes the flow of the game or a song so successful. This is how to excel in karaoke.

KEY POINT: The trick to making a smooth vocal transition is by using a combination of both head and chest tones when you begin the change-over. And the only way to improve on this aspect of singing is to practice your scales. As before, start low and with an open tone like *ah*. Think *do, re, me, fa, so* and back down while singing *ah*.

When you've done the first set, sing another set of *ahs* but start a little higher than you did the last time. Repeat this until you notice that you're moving from a chest tone to head tone. And when you listen to other singers, try to determine if what you're hearing is a chest or head tone or something in their transitional phase.

In Hawaii, many people live in the suburbs and commute to work for 30 minutes to an hour each way. Some of my students make good use of this time to practice their vocal exercises. Of course, it doesn't work quite as well if you use mass transportation like the bus. But it does if you're in a car.

Spend some time practicing transitions and imagine using a combination of both your chest and head tones, as well as a little throat. The transitional phase generally lasts for two-three notes. With time, practice and patience, your vocal transition, too, can become an estuary of head and chest tones. Once you move through that transitional stage, your high notes should be all head tones.

As before, relax your jaw and open up your throat when singing high notes with a head tone. Imagine aiming that sound to the top of your head. Fill your mouth and sinus cavities with sound.

RX

Just as putting a song in the right key can make someone sound better immediately, so, too, will common sense. Remember, your voice is like the rest of the muscles in your body. If you want to give it the best opportunity to perform as well as it's capable of, treat it the same way you would any other muscle.

If your throat gets dry before you sing - from nerves, air conditioning, or smoke in the room - suck on a piece of candy that has citric acid in it. The citric acid will help to draw out moisture.

And if you smoke, consider quitting or cutting back. There are volumes of books about the damage smoking causes your respiratory system.

KEY POINT SUMMARY

- Practice, practice, practice.
- Choose songs that fit your range.
- Determine the right key for your songs.
- Work on your transitions.

Chapter 5
Scale Your Way To Success

*"Good teaching is one-fourth preparation
and three-fourths theatre."
- Gail Godwin -*

Another question I'm asked in my karaoke classes is, "How do I keep from running out of air when I sing?"

It's pretty simple. Remember when you were a kid and blew out the candles on your birthday cake? Your stream of breath was probably pretty wide, sometimes even wet, and you used up your air very quickly. That was OK for five or six candles. But, extinguishing 30-40 candles before running short of air or setting off the smoke alarm requires greater breath control.

Instead, imagine blowing through a straw. Not only would you blow out the candles but you'd have air to spare. This is the kind of breath control you want to aim for while singing.

HOLD A LIGHT TO YOU

One way to check your breath control is to light a household candle and hold it about six inches from your mouth while singing. Be careful! Watch your eyelashes! If you're using the proper amount of air, the flame will barely flicker as you sing. If the flame dances, you're using too much air.

Hold a lit candle about six inches from your mouth while singing to measure breath control. If done properly, the candle will not flicker.

KEY POINT: Start off singing the scales by singing *oo* in a low, comfortable range, while thinking *do, re, me, fa, so, fa, me, re, do.* Hold *so* for five beats (count them in your head) before coming back down the scale. As you're holding *so*, imagine blowing through that straw.

Do the exercise again, this time starting a little higher than you did the last time and singing the same *oo* sound. Keep repeating this, each time starting a little higher than you did the last time and go as high as is comfortable for you.

When you're reached the top of your range, start the exercise all over again from the bottom, but this time with an *ah* sound. Continue imagining that you're blowing through a straw while sustaining that top note. As before, gradually work your way higher and higher.

When you're finished with *ah*, do the same with the other vowel sounds - *ei, oh,* and *ee*. And as with *oo* and *ah*, keep reminding yourself that you're blowing through a straw.

KEY POINT: Why work out on all these different vowel sounds? First, because every note you sing will have a vowel sound. Second, you'll discover that it's more difficult to control your breath on open sounds like *ei* and *ah* than on the closed ones like *oh, ee* and *oo*. It's harder to control your breath because your mouth is open wider on *ei* and *ah*.

While doing these exercises, also pay attention to your volume. Try to keep it consistent from the closed sounds like *oh, ee* and *oo* to the open ones like *ah* and *ei*. As you practice this exercise gradually lengthen the time you hold the top vowel sounds to 10, then 15 and then 20 beats.

Keep reminding yourself that you're blowing through that straw as you're holding out the vowel sound. You'll find that you'll be able to hold that top note longer as you gain more control over your breath.

Brian, a former student of mine, spends a lot of time free diving in Hawaii's crystal-clear waters. He told me that since he began singing karaoke and practicing breath control he can now free dive down to 60 feet, 20 feet deeper than before. Isn't that great? You can experience similar success too. Remember, practice is the key to improvement.

WHOLE LOTTA SHAKIN' GOING ON
There are many things that separate a mediocre singer from

a good one. Most professional singers not only sound good, but they also employ an extra technique or two.

One such enhancement is vibrato. In class, I sometimes need to make a clear distinction between vibrato - a wave, pulse or undulation in the voice - to vibrator, an occasional and spicy topic of Dr. Ruth's.

There are several types of vibrato depending on where and how the vibrato is produced. I discuss two in my karaoke classes. The type commonly taught by voice teachers is an abdominal vibrato. Vibrato produced by the abdominal muscles is the most controllable type. It can be turned on or off or speeded up or slowed down.

American pop singers often end a phrase in a slow song with a straight tone (one with no vibrato) and add the vibrato after a beat or two. Listen for it the next time you turn on the radio or hear a singer.

If you're a fan of legendary singers such as Misora Hibari from Japan or Edith Piaf from France, you'll hear a different type of vibrato. Their vibrato is produced by the vibration of their vocal cords. It's characterized by being fast and is almost always on. You hear vocal chord vibrato in some country- western singers also.

Some of my students show up in class with natural abdominal vibratos and others with natural vocal chord vibratos. They're fortunate, even though most of them haven't a clue as to how they acquired it. So how do you develop an abdominal vibrato if you don't yet have it? It takes work, practice and perseverance.

Remember how we checked our support by placing our fingertips under our lowermost rib? Do that again and cough. Those same muscles that provide our support also help produce the vibrato.

THE WAVE

Let's start off easy with just one pulse. Anyone can do that! We're going to precede each note by saying *sssss*, the sound a leaky radiator or a punctured tire makes.

KEY POINT: With your fingertips in position, find a note that's comfortable for you, take a breath and then sing one set of *hey* preceded by singing *ssssss* three times each. So you should be singing *ssssss, hey, ssssss, hey, ssssss, hey* on whatever note you've chosen.

If you're performing this exercise properly, you should feel slight pressure against your fingertips, at least on each *ssssss* and *hey*. Remember to maintain proper support throughout this exercise.

Now, with one pulse or wave out of the way, let's try for three. As before, perform one set of three repetitions each of *ssssss* followed by *hey*. Gradually work your way up from three to five, then seven and ten pulses or waves.

If you don't get it the first, second or tenth time, don't fret. Keep working at it. Good things take time. Remember to be a critical listener of other singers - not to criticize them - but to become more aware of what you're hearing. Is that abdominal or vocal cord vibrato you're hearing ?

As you get better at your vibrato, practice singing a slow song. Try holding a note, first without the vibrato, then with it. Then try hitting the note without any vibrato and, while you're holding it, add the vibrato.

GUSTO

Another technique that helps make singers more interesting is their ability to raise or to lower their volume. Remember back in school, sitting in class struggling to stay awake while the instructor spoke in a monotone voice?

Achieving volume control is a matter of increasing or decreasing one's air pressure while singing.

Pick up a whistle and blow it. You can vary the volume by increasing or decreasing your air pressure in the same way. Increase the pressure and you get louder. Decrease it and you get softer. Do the same with your voice.

KEY POINT: Remember our exercise - *do, re, me, fa, so* - and back down the scale singing different vowel sounds? Do it again, only this time, start off with an *ah* sound. Find a note in your lower range that's comfortable for you. But instead of singing in one volume, start off softly and gradually increase your volume and air pressure while going up the scale so that you're singing loudly at *so*. Hold *so* for about five or six beats before going back down the scale. When you do descend, gradually decrease your volume and air pressure. As in all your vocal exercises, practice on all the different vowel sounds - *ah, ei, oh, oo,* and *ee*. Stay in a comfortable range. It's not necessary to work your way higher and higher up the scale for this exercise.

KEY POINT: You may discover that it's easier to perform this exercise on the more open sounds like *ah* than on the closed ones like *oh, oo* and *ee*. That's because your mouth and

and throat are naturally open on these sounds.

But there should still be some space (about a half inch) between your upper and lower teeth while singing these closed vowels. What's important to remember in performing this exercise is to maintain proper support, particularly while singing softly. Of course, you should have support at all times.

But it's more difficult singing under control softly than belting out a tune. This exercise will help you do both while being in control.

MIKEY LIKES IT!

Another way to control your volume is by moving the microphone away from your mouth. I don't like to teach this but know of some students who are adept at controlling their volume this way. Again, practice makes perfect.

KEY POINT: No matter how you elect to control your volume, you will be singing into a microphone and there is a right way to use it. Many newcomers to karaoke are so nervous they use a death grip on the microphone. As nervous as you may be, don't do this because this tension will also be transferred to your shoulders and throat. My friend, recording artist Audy Kimura, has more to say about the proper use of a mike in Chapter 8.

Most of us also tend to be lazy when we talk. We really don't enunciate or open our mouths enough or as much as we think we do. Not only does this carry over into singing for most of us, but it's even more critical to pronounce each consonant clearly. I'm continuously amazed at how often I must remind students to open up their mouths a lot more. After all, we all open our mouths to talk, don't we, and feel we're opening up enough.

KEY POINT: When you sing, it's important to remember to enunciate even more than you normally do in your everyday speech. Slurring words may have worked for the late comedian-singer Dean Martin, but it's not effective for you. An audience will never get your message if you don't pronounce your consonants clearly.

Yes, it will feel like you're overdoing things but that's what is necessary when you're on a stage or singing in front of others.

HEY, LOOK ME OVER!

Still don't believe me? Choose a passage from a song, preferably one that ends with an *ah* or *ei* sound, like *Eiiiiiii,* like "I did it my waaaaaaaay." Now, stand in front of a mirror and watch your mouth as you sing it again, making sure to relax and drop your jaw and open up your mouth a lot more. Sound different? Sound fuller?

KEY POINT: Now, sing *ah,* and imagine that you're yawning on that top note while continuing to bear down with your support. Try it. Hear the difference? We've learned about volume control, vibrato, and breath control. In the next chapter, we focus on lyric analysis and gestures.

KEY POINT SUMMARY

- Imagine blowing through a straw to control your breath.
- Develop an abdominal vibrato.
- Perfect your volume control.
- Hold the microphone at a 45 degree angle and about 2-3 inches from your mouth.
- Enunciate your consonants.
- Imagine yawning on open sounds such as *ah* for fullness.

Chapter 6
Learn From The Pros

*"Do the thing you fear most and the
death of fear is certain."*
- Mark Twain -

There are a lot of good singers out there but only a handful of great performers. What's the difference between the two? A good singer is someone whom you might as well listen to on the radio or CD. You don't get any more enlightened by going to one of their concerts.

On the other hand, a great performer is someone who successfully brings together the added dimensions of sight, sound and presence to enthrall. Audiences are engaged and captivated because the performers are fully immersed in their songs. They fascinate their audiences and share that electric feeling of the moment with them. It's also the excitement that's in the air which you experience at a sporting event that you don't get from watching it on television.

Remember Rex Harrison as Dr. Doolittle in the movie, *My Fair Lady*? Or Glenn Close as Norma Desmond in the Broadway hit, *Sunset Boulevard*? Both are excellent actors but I don't believe either one is a trained singer.

What made their performances outstanding was that they were able to capture the feeling of their songs and effectively convey it to audiences through their voices, faces and body language.

Remember the last time you picked up the telephone and called a department store, airline office or hospital? Couldn't you just tell from the sound of the person's voice on the other end if he or she was having a bad day? Yet others simply exude so much radiance and friendliness that you can almost see that person smiling over the telephone.

Back when we only had radio and no television, actors relied solely on their voices to convey the feeling of their words and thoughts. That was great if all that mattered was how they sounded, for the audiences listening to their radios at home or at work were enraptured by the magic of sound. But when you're standing and singing in front of others, performing on stage, or competing, how you look and what you do with your arms and face are equally important.

KEY POINT: Stand in front of a mirror, full length, if possible, and watch yourself singing. You'll see just how small a lot of those gestures are. Or, if you have a video camera, record and see for yourself. Can you and do you put a smile in your voice? What are you doing with your arms and hands? Are they expressing the emotion of the song or are they hanging at your sides like two bunches of bananas?

I DID IT MY WAY

Some people even suggest that ole blue eyes, Frank Sinatra, doesn't have that good a voice. I'm not going to get into that argument. But nearly everyone, even his critics, agrees that he does an outstanding job of interpreting the lyrics of his songs.

You can achieve the same kind of success, too, by applying a few simple rules. First, start off by writing down the words to your song and memorizing them. Learn to sing the song without looking at the TV screen.

KEY POINT: Ask yourself, if you had to put the meaning of the song on a bumper sticker, just what would you say? If you don't have the answer to that, go back and read the words to the song. Nearly every popular song has a single theme throughout.

Next, look at the words of your song and paraphrase each line in your own words without repeating what the lyrics say or paying any attention to the rhythm. Do all of this aloud as if you were communicating the message of the song to someone. Now, try singing the song and transferring into the song that same feeling you had in paraphrasing it.

OPEN UP!

Just as we've learned to emote and open up our voices, we must also open up our faces and bodies to fully communicate the songs we're singing. Think about the last time you got excited watching a performer. Was he laid back and crooning like Perry Como or using all of his physical attributes to connect with you?

KEY POINT: Get rid of that "neutral" face, the kind you see a lot on television news. Many news anchors and reporters show us a "neutral" or expressionless face as they deliver the news. "Open" your face. Think of the kind of face (and voice) you put on when you want to get a small baby to smile and react to you, or when you want to make friends with a dog or cat.

Make use of your arms and hands. If you're already comfortable making gestures when you talk, continue doing so when you sing. But make them even bigger and grander. Why? Because on stage or in a large room, motions that are confined and close to your body get swallowed and lost.

If you haven't used your arms and hands, analyze successful performers and borrow gestures that feel comfortable to you. Begin moving across the room or stage as you sing. Sometimes, making a deliberate turn at the start of a phrase helps to accent a particularly important part of a song.

BUT I'M NERVOUS

The Book of Lists ranks public speaking number one of the things people are most afraid. But I believe getting up and singing before others has to be even more stressful. I've discovered in my classes that students who are well-grounded in breathing and support and who are singing songs in the right key, have a lot more confidence than those who aren't familiar with the basics.

As in public speaking, performing often helps to lessen stage fright. It's normal to be nervous before singing but most of that tension disappears as soon as you begin. Turn that nervous energy into something positive by using it to express the passion of the song. And although many of us really believe people can see our knees knocking and our bodies shaking when we sing, that honestly isn't true.

Over the years, I've seen insurance clerks, medical technicians, and housewives who had never sung in front of others come to class and blossom into wonderful performers. Many have appeared on local karaoke contests, and some have even won! Just an ounce of knowledge makes a ton of difference in confidence.

You may find this hard to believe but audiences around the world are kind and supportive. They want you to succeed. They really do. It usually helps to know people in the audience and sing to them, although some of my students have told me that they'd rather sing before strangers. If you don't know anyone in the audience, you'll have no trouble finding warm, friendly faces on which to focus.

KEY POINT: When you're singing, focus on a few friendly faces, but embrace the entire audience. In other words, don't simply sing to people on one side of a room or look in one direction. After focusing on someone for a few phrases, move on to someone else. Share yourself and "work" the entire room even if you're really only focusing on a few people.

If you feel uncomfortable focusing on people in the audience, here's a trick. Look to the last row in the room and perform as though you're singing to a person back there. I recommend this technique to students who sing in competitions or shows and even weddings. It also works in nearly any other kind of situation, big or small.

IT'S ALL IN THE MIND

KEY POINT: Try this exercise the next time you sing. Physically isolate yourself before you go up to sing (even if you have to excuse yourself and go into a bathroom stall to do so). Close your eyes for a few minutes and visualize yourself confidently walking on stage and delivering a song. See your open face and your gestures. Hear your voice rise and fall.

Then go out and take the stage and put on a great performance. When you're done, bow or wave to the audience. Pause and bask in those few seconds of appreciation. Don't look like you're in a hurry to get off the stage or sit down. You may feel relieved that your performance is over but don't let it show.

Great performers have the ability to shift into high gear once they take the stage. I've had numerous students who, in daily life, are very mellow and relaxed. But once they learned to open up and express themselves while singing, you see a totally different persona on stage. They're like kids again, making believe - playing a role and, most importantly, having fun! After all, where else could you cut loose or gyrate without feeling foolish than while singing? At work? I doubt it.

KEY POINT SUMMARY

- Put more meaning into your song through lyric analysis.
- "Open" your face.
- Put a smile in your voice on happy songs.
- Open up your body and your gestures for more effectiveness.
- Focus on a few people in the audience.
- Use visualization to prepare yourself for an outstanding performance.

Chapter 7
My Way
Or Developing Your Own Style

*"I know only two tunes: one of them is Yankee Doodle
and the other one isn't."*
- Ulysses S. Grant -

What distinguishes your singing from anyone else's? It's your style or the lack of one.

KEY POINT: The easiest way to develop your own style is to choose a song and get a recording of it as done by the original artist. Then listen to how he or she handles certain phrases and words. Mimic those things the original artist does that you feel comfortable with.

When you've gotten the style down pat, move on to another song by a different artist and again mimic those stylings that suit you. If you repeat this method three or four times, and always with a different artist - taking a little from one singer and something else from another - you'll eventually come into your own style. Of course, if you want to simply sound like The King, then just listen to and mimic Elvis all the time and become another of those Elvis sightings. There's nothing wrong with that either.

KEY POINT: Be less predictable and make your song a lot more interesting. Instead of always singing on the beat, sometimes try starting a line a little earlier or later. Remember how boring and difficult it was to stay awake in class and listen to a teacher who spoke at length in the same volume and at the same meter? The same is true of singers.

The musical director for a theatre production I once sang in reminded me of the difference between "live" theatre and karaoke. In community theatre, it's not unusual to have different volunteer orchestra members each night. As a result, songs are sometimes slower or faster from one night to another. Singers have to adapt and be flexible.

On the other hand, karaoke is consistent and your song will play the same way each time and in your key! If you know the basics of singing, all you have to do is focus on your performance.

If you're singing a slow song, use different volumes to punctuate certain important phrases and add in your vibrato. As a general rule, hold out the vowel sound on notes that you sustain rather than the consonant. It sounds much better holding out the *ooo* rather than the *nnn* in moon, for example.

Now that you're armed with all these tips on singing better, there are a few more things you ought to know. Just as you take your car in for regular service, your voice also needs to be maintained.

VOICE CARE

Before singing, sip a little room temperature or warm water. Keep sipping it and hydrating yourself. You may add a slice of lemon to the water.

Stay warm. It's not uncommon to get invited to sing at a function, only to arrive there and find that the room is like a chill box. If you're not sure about the environment you're going to sing in, take a sweater or scarf along just in case. After all, you don't have to wear it but it's nice to have handy just in case.

Let's compare singing with athletics again. Baseball pitchers wear jackets when their team is at bat to keep their arms warm. Ballet dancers don leggings to keep their calves warm. You should keep your throat (and vocal chords) warm between songs.

And when you're not singing, take care of your voice by not yelling or screaming at rock concerts or at sporting events. Give your voice a rest for a few days if you've been singing a lot. You would do that for your legs if you had just run a marathon.

A singer's body is his or her instrument. In fact, the singer's body is the only musical instrument that is crucially dependent on the condition of its carrying case. Take care of it.

Don't smoke. Not only is smoking damaging to your lungs but it also decreases your lung capacity. Avoid smoke-filled places if possible. In response to this irritation from smoke, the body secretes excess mucus which, in turn, causes throat-clearing and coughing, two big no-no's for the harm hey do to the vocal folds.

Singers must also be scrupulous about their nutrition. Avoid salt, which dries out the throat, and dairy products, which cause excess mucus. To keep the vocal folds moist and supple, drink a lot of liquids. In addition, pass up the wine and liquor because they often have a drying effect.

When you're playing a sport and pull a muscle, what's one of the first things you do? Most of us apply ice on the injured area as soon as possible to keep the swelling down. Imagine the effect of a cold drink on your vocal chords. That's not

62 · Scott Shirai

something you want to do.

KEY POINT: If you're going to be singing at a special gath
ering, a wedding, party, etc., or are simply out to impress
your significant other with a song, forego the ice cold beer or
frozen daiquiri and drink something warm like tea before
you sing. It'll help warm your vocal chords as well as relax
you.

And remember: Sing with an open throat. You're invit
ing serious injury if you push your throat too much.

KEY POINT SUMMARY

- Create your own style by borrowing from
  several different singers.
- Vary your rhythm sometimes.
- Keep your vocal chords relaxed. Try
  drinking warm liquids.

Chapter 8
Sound Check

"When music fails to agree to the ear,
to soothe the ear and the heart and the senses,
then it has missed the point."
- Maria Callas -

Now that you understand how to sing properly, there's something else to consider if you want to improve your sound: your microphone and sound system, and what you do with it.

A lot of people think microphones, like man, are created equal but that's not true. Just listen to what Polydor recording artist Audy Kimura has to say on the importance of good sound. "A properly used microphone and mix of music and voice will make anybody, from the worst to the best singer, sound better."

This record producer, music composer and arranger, recording engineer, acoustical and sound systems consultant adds, "A good microphone and using it properly are important because you want your audience or, if you're in a contest, the judges, to hear you clearly. The second reason, which a lot of people don't realize, is that the way you sound on the microphone and the sound system is the way you hear yourself." And as we discussed earlier in this book, hearing is critical to improving and singing well.

Audy explains that if the sound is too soft, people tend to push from their throats and sometimes strain themselves. Or if the sound's too loud, singers may tend to sing too soft and not obtain that full sound and projection out of their voices.

If you're singing on a system that has too much echo or reverb, it may be difficult to find your intonation. If it's too bassy, it will be hard to hear your intonation and you're not going to be singing on key, according to Audy.

Ideally, you should be holding the mike about 2 to 3 inches from and slightly below your chin at a 45 to 60 degree angle. Audy explains that most microphones used in karaoke boxes and lounges are called dynamic microphones and by design they get bassier when a singer gets closer to the mike. If you have a thin voice, Audy suggests working closer to the mike like an inch or so away to produce a rounder sound. Experimenting is critical.

KEY POINT: Be aware of where the speakers in the room are and be careful not to stand in front of or point a mike toward one. Chances are you'll generate a lot of feedback. Audy suggests testing a mike but being careful not to thump on it with your fingers because it can actually damage the speakers.

The mix, that balance between the background music and your voice, is also very important because too low a background will make it seem like you're singing a cappella. On the other hand, if the music is too loud, you may either strain and force your voice or simply not be heard at all. Audy suggests that one way to experience and find good mix is to listen to recordings of other singers and pay close attention to how the recording was mixed - discover why the voice sounds good.

One thing that plagues some singers are syllabant S's or popping consonants. They're even more apparent on a good sound system. Audy suggests slightly angling the mike up to your mouth and not singing directly into it at those times.

"The microphone has a diaphragm," he explains, " and it's like a little circle about the size of a quarter. And the more directly you face into that, that's where the mike is most sensitive."

When shooting pool became popular, players began buying their own cue sticks and taking them into billiard parlors. Similarly, Audy suggests that if you're serious about singing, invest in a good microphone and take it with you whenever you sing.

"Most of the microphones in karaoke bars and boxes have been abused and used, handled and dropped, and screamed in. For $200, you can find a good microphone which will make a big difference in tone and quality."

And if you do decide to shop for your own mike, Audy says, "Look for a unidirectional, dynamic one. Some of the ones I would recommend are the Shure Beta 58 or something in the Electrovoice ND series."

When it comes to karaoke, technology is zooming along and there are all kinds of inventions and improvements being introduced everyday. One of the newer innovations is Leadsinger, a wireless microphone with key and tempo control and gives you the freedom to sing over your boom box, car stereo, home stereo - anywhere.

Songs, up to 30 of them, are on interchangeable song chips that fit in the microphone and their lyrics are in an accompanying book.

Another newcomer is Froglips, a product of Tune1000. Froglips features its own MIDI-harmony format and takes the singer's voice and shifts automatically to simultaneously sing perfect four-part background harmonies using the same singer's voice. Tune1000 is credited with establishing the .kar file format used in MIDI karaoke.

Progress in compressing video has enhanced the capability of the CD. The current form, MPEG-1 video, can be played on CD-I, video CD, PCs with MPEG cards, and video game players.

No money to go out and sing? If you have a personal computer and are hooked into the Internet, you can access numerous MIDI karaoke shareware files.

MIDI - Musical Instrument Digital Interface - allows all kinds of electronic musical instruments to communicate with each other while displaying the song's lyrics on the screen as you sing along. Key changes are also possible and you can even print out the words if you wish.

By far, the best I've found is Rogene Talento's computer karaoke home page. You'll find several different MIDI karaoke players and hundreds of songs. Other good web sites are M.D.R. Software's MIDI songs karaoke system, Vincenzo Palleschi's, Raphael Pungin's, or the Bandit's Music & Sound home pages. (See Appendix)

Turtle Beach Systems has a PC card that will enable you to record your voice directly onto your hard drive while you're singing MIDI karaoke and then play back the entire file with the full accompaniment and your voice. Like the karaoke of the '60s, it, too, has a bouncing ball to help guide you through the song.

Whatever the format you may use for singing and whether or not it's before an audience, karaoke is definitely here to stay. It's a great way to reduce stress and a terrific way to make friends while having fun.

KEY POINT SUMMARY

· Don't stand in front of speakers or point your microphone at them.
· Invest in our own microphone.

Chapter 9
The Magic Of Karaoke

"Imagination is the highest kite that one can fly."
- Lauren Bacall-

When I started writing this book, I thought I'd simply share with you the same instruction I give my students. But one particular incident reminded me that karaoke lessons often result in more than just singing well.

I perform a lot of volunteer work in the community which includes putting on free karaoke workshops. One such session was for Winners At Work, a nonprofit group that helps train and place mentally challenged individuals in jobs. After a sing along, the executive director commented to me about how certain individuals who were usually withdrawn and shy suddenly emerged from their shells and sang with confidence.

I then reflected about other sing alongs I had led and realized that karaoke is indeed magical and has many other benefits. A check with KJs and other professionals quickly confirmed that. Here are some of their stories.

Bob Iinuma and his brother Don opened the Hawaii Multimedia Center in 1993 after managing a few nightclubs and restaurants since 1976 that offered karaoke. Bob says he's noticed that karaoke seems to click more for people who have a positive outlook, and definitely has an advantage for employers. "The way I look at it is, if you can sing together, you can work together," he adds. "If you cannot work together, I don't think you can sing together." Bob sees a lot more companies using karaoke to bring employees closer.

And karaoke has made people who look like wallflowers or who aren't particularly handsome more appealing, according to Bob. "If they're a great singer," Bob comments, "people are going to look at that person differently. They might become more attractive if you like their voice."

For some, karaoke has other benefits. Bob relates a story about a community college counselor who credits karaoke for relieving his stress and turning his life around. Tania Phan has been with Hawaii Stars Studios, Hawaii's biggest chain of boxes, since 1991. She tells a story of a female attorney who rents a room every Saturday and sings for an hour to relieve her stress from work. "Everybody always leaves happy," she remarks.

Don tells another story of a husband and wife who visited Hawaii Multimedia Center. This guy told Don that it was his mission in life to visit every karaoke place in Hawaii. Hawaii Multimedia Center happened to be the 177th karaoke place he had visited. The visitor, who had suffered a stroke four years earlier, said that his doctor prescribed singing, and that karaoke had helped heal him.

Hawaii's Al Waterson is a professional singer, recording artist and actor who got into karaoke in 1981 in Hawaii. He was the first to provide a stage, lights, and song lists for karaoke singers and is presently a KJ at Oahu's Fisherman's Wharf restaurant.

He's encouraged hundreds of singers to come on stage over

the years and has seen how this popular pastime has even meant dramatic career changes for some.

"We've seen people start out singing karaoke with no intention of becoming professional singers," said Al and Nancy Bernal, promotions manager for Al Waterson & You Entertainment.

Al recalls meeting someone years ago who was terribly shy and had trouble carrying a tune. But through a lot of hard work and determination, that person not only sings well, he also gets paid to impersonate Stevie Wonder in a local showroom.

Nancy recounts how singing even made a mail carrier a celebrity along his route. "When he first came to sing he was so nervous it showed all over his face. Karaoke has built up such confidence in him that has carried

Al Waterson

over into his everyday life. On his route now, he's known as the singing postman."

The mail carrier's entire family has since taken up singing as well and Al says he's seen that activity draw the family and many others closer together.

Psychologically, karaoke also seems to have its benefits. Al shares how people from groups like Parents Without Partners drop into Fisherman's Wharf and re-establish their confidence in relationships through singing.

It seems every KJ has a success story to tell. Annie Stephens is a KJ at another popular Oahu night spot, Beacon's Restaurant. She tells of one customer who, when he first started singing, was so shy he wouldn't talk to anyone. "Now he makes his way around the room and talks to everyone who comes in and is even recording an album now."

Mike McCartney, along with Carole Kai and Dirk Fukushima, are the co-creators of *Hawaii Stars*, a popular weekly karaoke television show. Mike says he got the idea for the show after seeing his shy, reticent father-in-law transform into a confident outgoing guy through karaoke. And since the show's beginnings in March 1993, Mike says he's also witnessed the same conversion with many of the singers who have appeared on the show. "When I see them on the street afterwards, their whole essence has changed."

According to Mike and Carole, the show is not about winning or losing, but about helping folks become better people by believing in themselves. Mike says one of the biggest examples of that was in Kealii Reichel who appeared on the show, did not win, but went on to record several albums, including the best selling album in Hawaii. Reichel was also nominated for a Grammy Award.

Carole, co-host of the show, remarks that it has given many people more confidence, poise and self-esteem. "One of our contestants was a woman who had been abused by her husband and had very low self-esteem. As the woman sang her way up to the finals, I saw how each show progressively helped rebuild her confidence and life."

The popularity of *Hawaii Stars* prompted Carole and Mike to start *Keiki Stars*, a television show aimed at young people. Keiki is Hawaiian for child. Carole says the show is successful because every child is made to feel like a winner.

An even older television show, *Kidioke*, has been airing on Honolulu's Oceanic Cablevision since 1987. Producer Pauwilo Look, shares how there are countless youngsters who have appeared on the show and later went on to become successful in theatre and television.

"More importantly, the kids all gain a lot of confidence and experience," she says. "There's one incident I'll never forget because it demonstrates the resolve and confidence of the kids. While one of our winners was singing she tripped over a microphone cable. Instead of losing her composure, this 11-year-old had the poise and presence of mind to lay on the stage and continue singing. And, when she was done, she just got up and dusted herself off. The audience was ecstatic," Pauwilo adds.

Walter Omori has been producing the *Country Music Karaoke Contest* since 1971 and is also the owner of Walter's Karaoke and Sound in Honolulu. He's been a KJ since 1983 and has seen how perseverance has paid off for many singers. He recalls one instance in which he first heard a local flight attendant sing.

"Her voice was soft, pleasant and not impressive," said Walter, "but after nearly a year of practice, she placed second in the contest. She took the top prize the following year and now sings with a band."

Walter recalls the many people that come into his store and share how their kids stay home more often and sing since they purchased a karaoke system. "I've seen many families brought closer together," he adds.

Socially, karaoke is also popular for making new friends. "We've seen individuals come to the club solo and all of a sudden they end up singing together. We've seen marriages come out of some of these situations," Al and Nancy agree, calling this matchmaking karaoke.

OK, now that we've seen how karaoke can positively affect lives, pull out your tape recorder. Tape yourself singing the same song you sang when you started reading this book. Listen to your original recording and compare the two. Notice the difference? Hear the improvement? Keep practicing and working out vocally. You'll get even better. And, if you want my personal evaluation, please check out the special offer you'll find on Page 89.

Singing has always been around and always will be. It is a universal language and has been loved by people throughout the world. I wrote this book because I love singing and you probably bought it for the same reason.

Look at recorded history. It is overflowing with examples of people, their instruments, and their music dating as far back as prehistoric times. And this ongoing love affair with singing has helped to nurture the development and eruption of karaoke as we know it today.

Wherever the forum or whatever the format, karaoke has a positive influence on the lives of people around the world. It can and it will for you if it hasn't already. It's fun. It will bolster your confidence in your job and daily life. Why, it may even lead to a career change.

Good luck and enjoy many more years of great singing!

Appendix

Glossary

Box: An outlet that rents privately-equipped rooms in which persons can sing karaoke.

Chest Tone: A tone produced by the resonance of the chest, characterized by its richness and fullness.

Compact Disc & Graphic (CD+G): A 5" compact disc (CD) containing the music and the lyrics to a song. The music can be heard over any CD Player. However, if the lyrics (words) to a song are to be displayed over a television set, a special karaoke player is required. These discs usually contain 10 or more songs.

DJ: Disc jockey.

Free Tone: The sound produced by singing with one's jaw dropped and relaxed; also referred to as an open throat.

Hardware: The equipment necessary to amplify, play or record music.

Head Tone: A tone produced in the mouth and sinus cavities, it is characterized by its brightness.

Karaoke Box: See box.

KJ: Karaoke jockey - a DJ who sings, too.

Laser Disc: A 12" disc containing the lyrics (words) and music of a song with a video playing on screen in the background. These discs usually contain from 14 to 28 songs.

Multiplex: A lead vocal is recorded on one channel to guide the singer while the other channel contains the music. This is controlled by the balance control of your sound system.

Octave: Going from *do* up to *do*; i.e.,*do, re, mi, fa so, la, ti, do.*

Pitch Control: Also known as Key Changer, Key Controller, and/or Digital Key Changer. This allows you to vary the pitch (range) of the song you are singing. A pitch control varies the tempo and pitch while Digital Key Changers only vary the pitch and not the tempo.

Range: The reach of one's voice - from low to high and vice versa.

RF Modulator: An adapter that converts the line signal (RCA Jack) to a coaxial signal (Coax Post) from a karaoke player allowing it to play on any TV.

Software: The media (disc or tape) used to store and play recorded information such as music, video and song lyrics.

Song Films: Silent films that featured a ball that bounced over words to songs so that audiences could sing along.

Straight Tone: The absence of vibrato in a sustained note.

Superimpose: Allows you to display a video input from a VCR, video camera or TV behind the lyrics of a compact disc & graphic (CD+G).

Support: The bearing down of the abdominal muscle which, combined with proper breathing, is the foundation of good singing.

Vibrato: The wave or pulse in a held note, the most preferable kind coming from the abdomen.

Video CD: A 5" compact disc (CD) with a video back ground. These discs offer laser features in a smaller and more compact size. These discs require a video CD player and will not play on existing laser disc players.

Vocal Masking: Also known as Vocal Partner/Voice Cancel, this feature will mute the recorded vocal on a multiplex recording when you begin singing into the microphone and brings them back when you stop.

Vocal Reducer: Also known as Vocal Masking/Vocal Suppressor, it reduces vocal track on any non-karaoke compact disc or cassette tape. At times this may lower instruments in the same range.

Resources

Recommended Reading

Alderson, Richard. *Complete Handbook of Voice Training.* West Nyack: Parker Publishing, 1979.

Chun~Tao Cheng, Stephen. *The Tao of Voice.* Rochester: Destiny Books, 1991.

Gonda, Jr., Thomas A. *Karaoke: The Bible.* G-Man Publishing, Oakland, CA, 1993

Hewitt, Graham. *How to Sing.* New York: Taplinger Publishing, 1978.

Hines, Jerome. *Great Singers on Great Singing.* New York: Limelight Editions, 1994.

Howard, Elisabeth & Austin, Howard. *Born To Sing.* Tarzana: 1985.

Howard, Elisabeth & Austin, Howard. *Sing Like A Pro.* Los Angeles, 1989.

Kosarin, Oscar. *The Singing Actor.* Englewood Cliffs: Prentice Hall, 1983.

Silver, Fred. *Auditioning For The Musical Theatre.* New York: Penguin Books, 1985.

Stone, Jerald B. *You Can Sing.* New York: Amsco, 1995.

Sutherland, Susan. *Singing.* Lincolnwood: NTC Publishing, 1995.

Good Starter Songs

Just starting out? Try these songs with limited ranges.

After the Lovin'

At the Hop

Can't Help Falling in Love

Could I Have This Dance?

Diana

Everybody Loves Somebody

Five Hundred Miles

Release Me

The Rose

Sweet Someone

Tequila (That's a joke)

The Ten Commandments of Karaoke

When you go out to karaoke in a club or bar, there is an unspoken etiquette that should be observed. Doc Laing, a DJ and KJ in the Denver area shared these 10 commandments which I've amended slightly.

Commandment #1
THOU SHALL NOT jeer, heckle, boo, harass, or otherwise interrupt a singer. It's not only bad manners, but depending on the crowd, you may experience anything from a lot of nasty looks to a very quick exit out of the bar. Be supportive!

Commandment #2
THOU SHALL NOT get drunk if you are planning to perform. The equipment used for karaoke is expensive, and if you were to cause an accident resulting in damage, you may be held accountable.

Commandment #3
THOU SHALL NOT whine about when your next turn is. If a good KJ is working the place, he or she will be fair about the schedule, and you will sing no less than everyone else. Granted, there are those who will favor their friends and co-KJs, and if you run across one of these, go someplace else where you will be treated better. Their loss right?

Commandment #4
THOU SHALL NOT be upset if another patron sings a song you were planning to sing. There are usually plenty of songs to choose from, and you can always do it another night.

The first KJ I ever knew, always knew her regulars and their favorite songs. If there were any duplicate songs coming up, she would ask you if you wanted to change your selection, or sing it right after the other, as a sort of challenge.

Commandment #5

THOU SHALL NOT use foul language when at the mike. It might be suitable at Joe's Cave, but most places find it very UNacceptable. You might find it is the last time on-stage for you.

Commandment #6

THOU SHALL NOT swing the mike or dance with the mike stand. Please have respect for the equipment, and be aware of the space available for your performance. That mike cord will only go so far you know.

Commandment #7

THOU SHALL NOT sing along louder than the performer. This can be very irritating, and is a lesson I learned first hand. The guy handed me the mike and told me to finish the song. VERY embarrassing!!

Commandment #8

THOU SHALL NOT join in with a singer unless you are invited. This could also be very embarrassing, and is no way to make friends.

Commandment #9

THOU SHALL NOT carry on a loud conversation next to the stage. Most bars have limited space, and you will find the stage is sometimes close to some tables. If the sound is not right, it is hard to follow the song cues and such when you have people talking loudly next to you.

Commandment #10

THOU SHALL APPLAUD!! Come on now, anyone who gets up there deserves some attention, don't you think? And besides, we're all here to have fun!!

Karaoke Publications

American Karaoke Magazine
538 Village Dr. #4598
Pagosa Springs, CO 81147
email: KARAOKEONE@AOL.COM

Karaoke Scene
18149 Ventura Blvd. #240
Tarzana, CA 91356
email: KSCENE@aol.com

Karaoke USA
2140 Shattuck Ave., Suite 2139
Berkeley, CA 94704
email: KaraokeUSA@aol.com

Mobile Beat
P.O. Box 309
Rochester, NY 14445

Web Page Resources

Bandit's Music & Sound Page
http://netsys.syr.edu/~mtwoodwa/music.htm

Big Fish Records - Christian Karaoke
http://www.bigfish.com/

Bonsai's JPop Page
http://www.its.newnham.utas.edu.au/users/bkidd/jpop/
jpop.html

CD+G Karaoke Software
http://www.karaokeusa.com/cdsw.html

Computer Karaoke Homepage
http://www.teleport.com/~labrat/karaoke.shtml

Golden Oldies
http://www.coach4u.com/oldies.htm

Jeff's Songwriting & Midi Center
http://www.west.net/~midiman/jeff1.html

Karaoke U
http://www.hits.net/~karaokeu
Scott Shirai's Web Site

Karaoke Midi: Midi Songs Karaoke System Home Page
http://www.pangeanet.it/~mdr/

Karaoke Music Mazha!!!
http://www.best.com/~cheriss/karaoke.htm

Karaoke Nite
http://www.han.com/karaoke/index.html

Karaoke Page
http://www.servtech.com/public/sobeit/karaoke.html

Karaoke Plus
http://www.web2000.net/karaoke/

Karaoke Products - VHS Tapes, CD's & Cassette Tapes
http://www.primenet.com/~karaoke/prichome.html

KaraokeWOW! The Internet Karaoke Store© Online Catalog
http://www.primenet.com/~karaoke/welcome.html

Home Page for Doc Laing
http://home.aol.com/doclaing

Looney Tunes Karaoke-Home
http://www.kids.warnerbros.com/karaoke/

Matt's COOL Links
http://netsys.syr.edu/~mtwoodwa/links.htm

M.D.R. Software
http://www.pangeanet.it/~mdr/

Mobile Beat-The DJ Magazine-Rochester,NY
http://www.mobilebeat.com/

Sound Choice Karaoke Software
http://www.soundchoice.com/karaoke/

Sun Fly Karaoke CD+G List
http://www.karaokeusa.com/cdg/sf.html

Thai Karaoke Music
http://guide-
p.infoseek.com/NN/IS/frames/
DB?2,,A376949,qt=karaoke&col=NN&st=20
&rt=NA

Thuy Nga Video Home Page
http://www.vweb.net/thuynga/

Rogene R. Talento's Homepage
http://www.teleport.com/~labrat/

White Pine Software
http://www.wpine.com/

Widow's Web
http://wilkes1.wilkes.edu:80/~zimmerja/

NEWSGROUPS:
alt.music.karaoke

Please send me Scott Shirai's book:
Karaoke: Sing Along Guide to Fun & Confidence

NAME: _____

ADDRESS: _____

CITY, STATE, ZIP: _____

PHONE: _____ FAX: _____

<u>TOTAL COPIES ORDERED:</u> _____

($10.95 + .46 tax = <u>$11.41 per book</u>) $_____

S&H: <u>Priority Mail</u> 1-2 Books @ $3
3-5 Books @ $6
ADD <u>S&H</u> $_____

AMOUNT ENCLOSED: (U.S. $) $_____

☐ Check or Money Order ☐ VISA ☐ MasterCard

_____ Exp. Date _____

Signature: _____

SEND TO:
Visual Perspectives • P.O. Box 459 • Honolulu, HI 96809

☐ **Please check here if you would like your book(s) autographed.**

An Offer You Can't Refuse!

I am pleased to offer purchasers of *Karaoke: Sing Along Guide To Fun & Confidence* the opportunity to submit a cassette tape of one song for private evaluation and consultation.

Please complete the coupon below and submit it along with your cassette (in its protective case), a money order or cashier's check for $10 (U.S.) and a business-sized, self-addressed envelope with proper return postage to:
Visual Perspectives, P.O. Box 459, Honolulu, HI 96809.

NAME: _____

ADDRESS: _____

_____

CITY, STATE, ZIP: _____

_____

Title of Song:_____

How long singing karaoke? _____ Years
<u>Comments:</u>

Your tape will be returned within 30 days.

About *the* Author

Scott Shirai may be the only person in captivity to be teaching karaoke at an American university. He has been teaching the popular subject in the University of Hawaii system since 1989, as well as at Hawaii Multimedia Center and various locations of Hawaii Stars Studios throughout Hawaii.

He majored in music (voice) at the university's Manoa campus, has sung professionally, appears on stage in Honolulu, and has been a judge for numerous karaoke contests.

Shirai works full-time as Director, Community Relations for Hawaiian Electric Industries (HEI), a large diversified holding company based in Honolulu. Among his duties are responsibilities for media and public relations. Prior to joining HEI, he worked more than 10 years in radio and television news as a reporter, executive news producer, morning anchor, and news director.

He has spoken on the mainland before the Edison Electric Institute, Public Relations Society of America (PRSA) and Center for Corporate Community Relations at Boston College and presented workshops for the State of Hawaii, University of Hawaii and Kapiolani Community College on effectively communicating with the news media and on crisis communications.

Shirai is an accredited public relations professional and has been a national delegate and chapter president for the Hawaii Chapter of the Public Relations Society of America. In addition to teaching karaoke, he teaches video production, video editing and political election courses at the University of Hawaii.

* * * * *